MARK NICHOLAS
THE LOST HORSE

For Pippi & Amelie.
Every page turned is one more adventure you'll share x
M. N.

First published in 2018 by order of the Tate Trustees
by Tate Publishing, a division of Tate Enterprises Ltd,
Millbank, London SW1P 4RG

www.tate.org.uk/publishing

A catalogue record for this book is available from the British Library

ISBN 978 1 84976 5657

Distributed in the United States and Canada by ABRAMS, New York
Library of Congress Control Number applied for
Printed in China by Toppan Leefung Printing Ltd
Colour reproduction by Evergreen Colour Management Co. Ltd, Hong Kong

REWARD
MISSING
The LOST HORSE
LOST HORSE
MISSIN
PRICELESS
52 YEARS OLD
IN THE GALLERY
PLEASE HELP

People came from far and wide to see the sculpture of
the man and his horse. Legend had it that the sculpture
changed position when no one was looking.

It always drew a big crowd . . . that was
until the day the horse vanished.

But where had he gone?
Gigantic bronze sculptures don't just disappear!

The horse was very valuable and he had to be found quickly.
Detectives looked for clues. They searched far and wide,
but he was nowhere to be seen.

They searched the city and all of the surrounding villages.

The news spread quickly throughout the land,
but no sign of the horse could be found.

Deep in the forest stood a house taller than any of the trees
surrounding it. This was the home of a young girl called Lyra.
Her house was so far from the nearest village
that she often felt very lonely.

Sitting in her bedroom, Lyra would spend her time daydreaming.
Her favourite dream was of having her very own horse.
It would be as white as snow, softer than a cloud, and they would
be the very best of friends.

Lyra wished she could have a horse,
even if it was only for one day.

One morning, just as Lyra was about to go down to breakfast,
she heard a tapping at her window.

She couldn't believe her eyes!

Lyra burst out
of her room
and ran down

and down,

and down.

"A horse!" she cried. "My wish came true!"

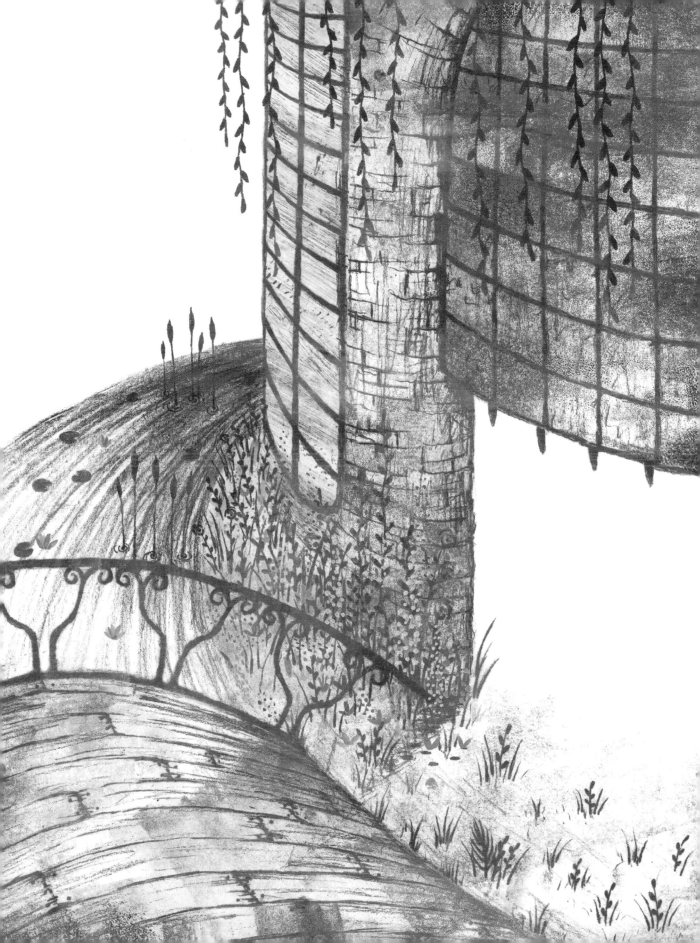

Lyra loved her new horse. He wasn't white, but his coat was
a beautiful bronze colour. Together they would go on long
walks through the forest, picking flowers as they went.

When Lyra's legs got tired, the horse would let her
up on to his back then race through the trees,
back home in time for tea!

At bedtime, Lyra would give him a bath and he would blow bubbles, which always made her laugh. Afterwards he loved it when she dried his ears with a towel. It tickled!

Every night, the horse slept
outside Lyra's bedroom window.

He was very careful not to snore.
Lyra had told him off about that before!

Lyra watched her horse until she fell asleep,
then she dreamed about all the wonderful
things they would do together when they woke up.

She just couldn't believe her luck.

Their days together were full of happiness.
However, every now and then, Lyra thought
the horse looked sad, as if he was missing something.

Lyra knew what that felt like.

"Let's play hide-and-seek again," she said.
It was the horse's favourite game
and Lyra knew it would cheer him up.

She began to count to ten.

"One, two, three, four . . ."

The horse went to hide,
but before Lyra reached five
she heard a rustling noise.

Lyra opened her eyes and saw a tall figure
walking towards the horse.

She didn't understand what was happening.

She listened really hard, but the man didn't
utter a single word. He stretched out his
arms and the horse walked over to him.

Suddenly Lyra knew what the horse was missing.
He was missing his friend.

The man embraced the horse gently.
Lyra couldn't watch. She knew why the man
had come. He had come to take the horse away.

Lyra suddenly felt very alone.

The horse glanced back. He lowered his head and nuzzled close to Lyra. She held him tightly.

"I didn't realise you were lost!" she sobbed. "But I understand. You need to go back home."

In a flash, the horse whipped Lyra up on to
his back and, together with the bronze man,
they sped away through the forest.

They raced straight past Lyra's house.
"Where are we going?" she cried.
But there was no answer.

Soon, the dense forest started to disappear,
and Lyra realised where they were going.

"The city!" she squealed excitedly.
"I've never been to the city before!"

Just as Lyra started to wonder why
they had come, the man pointed to a
building on the other side of the river.
It was the art museum.

"But how will we get there?" Lyra asked.
There were hundreds of people staring at
them and blocking their way.

Suddenly the man jumped into the river.
The horse followed, with Lyra still on his back.

They started to swim towards the museum.

On the other side, they climbed out of the river and Lyra looked up at the museum. She had seen it in her book and knew about the wonderful objects inside.

The bronze man climbed back inside the building. Lyra knew the horse would follow.

She jumped down from the horse's back and held him one last time.

"Thank you for being my friend," she said. "I love you!"

All around them, people were cheering and clapping.
Lyra couldn't believe what was happening. She had
found the lost horse sculpture. She was a hero!

Everyone knew her name!
Even the Queen personally thanked Lyra
for returning the sculpture to the gallery.

After the crowds had left, Lyra finally found
herself alone again with the man and his horse.

She couldn't leave without saying one final thing.

"Goodbye. I promise
I'll come back and
visit you often."

The End